cuscus

numbat

in this book

koala

crocodile

echidna

Mommy, Daddy, I Had a Bad Dream!

Written by Martha Heineman Pieper, Ph.D.

Illustrated by Jo Gershman

SMART L♥VE PRESS

MOMMY, DADDY, I HAD A BAD DREAM!
by Martha Heineman Pieper, Ph.D.

For permissions write:
Smart Love Press, LLC
400 E. Randolph Street, Suite 205
Chicago, IL 60601

Book design and cover design by Jo Gershman.
Illustrations are rendered in watercolor.

Summary: When Joey, a bouncy happy kangaroo, has a series of bad dreams,
his parents lovingly help him understand them. Children will be fascinated and
enlightened as Joey learns to make sense of his bad dreams and to put put himself back
to sleep feeling comforted and in charge.

Library of Congress Control Number: 2012900845
ISBN: 978-0-983-86640-4 (library binding)
First Edition: 2012
10 9 8 7 6 5 4 3 2 1

[1. Bad dreams—Juvenile fiction. 2. Nightmares—Juvenile fiction.
3. Sleep problems—Juvenile fiction. 4. Animal stories—Juvenile fiction.]

www.mommydaddyihadabaddream.com
www.smartlovepress.com

Printed in China

Ages three and up.

Joey was a happy little kangaroo who loved to bounce into bed, listen to stories with his baby sister, Jilly, have a big cuddle, and go to sleep with Clarissa, his pet cuscus, and Sammy, his fuzzy green wombat.

"Night, night, Joey. Sweet dreams. We love you!"

"Night, night."

But, one night
Joey had a bad dream.

Joey bounced straight into his parents' room.
"Mommy, Daddy, I had a terrible dream!
The judge said NO apples with honey
for three whole days! Why would
I have such a bad dream?"

"Let's think about it," Daddy said.
"Dreams are stories we tell ourselves for a reason.
We just have to understand the reason.
Are you upset about something that happened today?"

Joey thought. "Well, I was really mad when Mommy wouldn't play because she had to feed Jilly."

I wish my baby sister would go away!

Mommy cuddled Joey. "You know, all children feel angry when a little sister or brother takes Mommy's and Daddy's attention. You can be angry and still love us at the same time! Maybe you were worried about feeling angry. That's why you told yourself that dream where the judge was punishing you."

Joey nodded. "Hmmm — I see."

"Could you go back to sleep now?"

"Yes!" said Joey.

a few weeks later

"Night, night. Sleep well. We hope
you feel better. We love you!"

"Night, night. Sniffle, sniffle."

"Mommy, Daddy, I had a bad dream
that you wouldn't let me in!
I   am
very
UPSET!"

"That was a bad dream!" said Daddy. "It sounds scary."

"I hate these terrible dreams," said Joey. "It was horrible!"

Mommy asked, "Did anything upset you yesterday?"

I was too sick to go to Kenny Koala's birthday party. I wanted to slide down on my tail like all of my friends. I was really sad I missed it. It's not fair!

Daddy asked, "Did you feel locked out of the party by your
cold? Do you think that's why you dreamed you were locked
out of the house?"

Joey thought. "Yes...But why didn't you let me in?"

Mommy gave Joey a big hug. "Children think their parents
can do anything. Maybe you thought we could zap
your cold away so you could go to the party."

"Joey, no matter how much we love you,"
Daddy added, "We can't make your cold
go away like magic, even though we wish we could."

"So in my dream I told myself that you were keeping me
out, even though it was the cold," nodded Joey.

"Are you ready for us to tuck you back into bed?" asked Mommy.

"Yes, I am," Joey smiled.

"Night, night. We love you."

a few weeks later

I don't want to go to bed!

"Night, night. We love you."

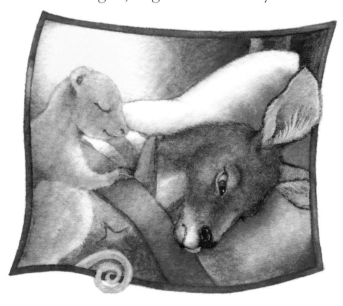

"Hmmph."

That night, Joey dreamed
that he grew
and **GREW**
and **GREW**
and played all night long.

"Daddy, can I have a hug?"

"I had a dream which was good because I was so big
I could do anything I wanted, but then it was terrible
because I was too big for a hug."

Mommy asked, "Can you think of something to explain that dream?"

Joey thought. "Well, I had to go to bed even though I didn't want
to, and if I were big you couldn't make me."

Daddy said, "You figured it out. Joey, that's terrific. Right now, even though you are too small to stay up late, you are the perfect size for lots of hugs and snuggles."

"Night, night. We love you."

"Night, night. Sleep well. We love you!"

"Night, night."

"Should I run to Mommy and Daddy for a hug?"

"Why would I dream you were missing?
Let's think about today. I was playing with Kenny."

"We couldn't agree what game to play, and he left."

"I was upset because Kenny left, so I dreamed that you left me too, Clarissa. That's it! Now we can go back to sleep. Night, night, Clarissa."

The next morning,
Joey bounced into the kitchen.

"Mommy, Daddy, I had a bad dream last night,
but I figured out WHY and I went back to sleep
and had a good dream!"
"Joey, great job!"

Night, night.

Acknowledgements

*This book is the product of Johanna Heineman-Pieper's gentle but
persistent request that I write for children as well as their parents.
Johanna, Thalia Field, and Victoria Stein contributed many inspired suggestions.
And special thanks to all the young "product testers," including Gershon and Benjamin.*

In memory of my mother, Natalie Goldstein Heineman.
Martha Heineman Pieper

*To my father and mother, Louis and Revelle,
who always came when I called in the night.*
Jo Gershman